THINGS PEOPLE DO

Anne Civardi

Illustrated by Stephen Cartwright

Designed by Roger Priddy

Consultant: Betty Root

CONTENTS

The Island of Banilla

This is the island of Banilla where all the people in this book live and work. It is not a very big island, but it has all the things the people who live here need. There is a hospital, an airport, schools, a hotel, restaurants, shops, farms, parks, a theatre, a bank, a fire station and a police station.

The mail that comes in to and goes out of the island is sorted at the post office in the town square. All the telephones are controlled from here as well.

The Mayor of Banilla is called Mayor Naze. She and her six councillors are in charge of the island. Lots of other people work for the island, too. They help to make it a clean, safe and healthy place to live.

Banilla National Flag

Banilla Stamp

Banilla Airport

Bani Telev...

Mayor Naze's House

Saint Havedoc Hospital

Town Hall

Banilla Ice cream Factory

Noah Lott School

Doctor Sillin's Surgery

The Blitz Hotel

Post Offic...

BA333

Banilla Orchid Plantation

Daisychain Farm

Mike Atsil's Surgery

Saint Lee Church

Gus O'Lean's Garage

The Daily Blaze

NEWSPAPER

Bunn's Bakery

Fire Station

Theatre

Bank

Police Station

Fish Market

The island workers

Every six years there is an election. The people of Banilla vote for a mayor and six councillors. Twice a week, the mayor meets the councillors in the town hall. They discuss any island problems and decide what to do about them.

Mayor   *Councillors*

The councillors have different jobs to do. They look after the schools in Banilla as well as buses, roads and the hospital. They also make sure that the houses and buildings are safe and that all the hotels and restaurants are clean.

Judge   *Police, Fire and Ambulance Officers*

Judge Fairley is head of the Banilla court of law. He makes sure people get a fair trial if they are accused of a crime. And he decides what punishment to give if they are found guilty. The Banilla police and fire brigade help to look after the people on the island.

Dustman   *Street Cleaner*   *Sewage Worker*

The dustmen, street cleaners, sewage workers, park keepers and gardeners also work for the island. They keep it clean and tidy. Engineers make sure that every house has clean water, electricity, gas and a telephone that works.

Engineers   *Postwoman*   *Park keeper*

The Fisherman

Frank and Freddy Flounder are fishermen. Early every morning, they set off from the harbour in their boat 'The Jolly Nearly'. It is hard and dangerous work out at sea.

The two brothers are very careful. They know where to find the rocks and strong currents around Banilla. Today, they will put out their nets about two kilometres from the shore.

Fisherman

Frank dresses into warm, waterproof clothes ready for a long and wet day at sea. His wife, Netta, makes him sandwiches and hot soup to take.

Coastguard

While Frank checks the fishing nets, Freddy talks to the coastguard. He finds out exactly what the weather will be like at sea today.

There is a special instrument called a fish finder aboard The Jolly Nearly. It shows the fishermen when there is a shoal of fish underneath or near their boat.

Catching fish

A basket on the rigging of the boat tells other boats to keep clear.

Frank hauls in the net when it is full of fish. Freddy scoops them up on to the deck.

The fish market

Every Tuesday and Friday, Frank and Freddy sell their catch at a big fish auction on the quayside.

Freddy wins a prize for catching the biggest lobster of the year.

Mayor

Some of the fish is canned for pet food or made into fish meal for fertilizer.

Porter

Freddy sorts the slippery fish into boxes and covers them with ice to keep them fresh.

At the end of the day, the fishermen head for home. They have caught many fish.

Back in the harbour, Frank unloads the boxes of fish and washes down his boat.

Catching lobsters

2

3

Freddy also catches lobsters. Once a week, he rows out to check his lobster pots.

Freddy has been lucky. The big lobster he has caught will fetch a good price at market.

Freddy puts fresh bait in the top of the lobster pot and drops it back into the sea.

Hotel keeper

Fish salesman

The fish salesman, Ed Zoff, moves up and down the rows of boxes calling out the fish prices.

Carmen Stay buys fish for a banquet at her hotel.

Sea Captain

7

The Builder

Manuel Laber is a builder. Eight skilled people work for him and help him build houses in Banilla. At the moment, they are building a smart new house for Mayor Naze.

Each of Manuel's team has a special job to do. Doug is the groundworker, Bill Ditt lays the bricks. Tim Burr is the carpenter and Hugh Bend the plumber.

Lotta Light is an expert electrician and Mick Swell a fine plasterer. Rufus does the tiling, while Matt's job is to paint and decorate.

Builder Plumber Electrician Brick-layer Carpenter Painter Tiler Plasterer Groundworker

Building a house

1

Before work begins, Manuel inspects the site Mayor Naze has chosen for her house. It is high on a hill overlooking the Banilla sea.

The house is finished. Mayor Naze and her husband are delighted. It is even better than they both expected.

The Mayor gives Manuel and his team a gold medal for their good work.

Maid

2

Architect

Albert Hall, the architect, has drawn designs to show how the house will look. Manuel follows these plans carefully as he builds the house.

3

At the builder's yard, Manuel orders the materials he needs to build the house. He buys bricks, cement, wood, nails, plaster, paint and tiles.

4

Doug is first on the site. With a big digger, he clears the ground and digs deep trenches for the drains and house foundations.

2 Flora Bunder, the landscape gardener, plants the garden with all the Mayor's favourite flowers, and, as a surprise, two big Banilla trees.

11 Matt Finish has painted the woodwork in Mayor Naze's bedroom and hung the wallpaper. He wipes off the splashes of wallpaper paste.

10 Rufus, the tiler, uses special terracotta tiles made in Banilla for the roof. Next he will lay different tiles in the two bathrooms.

Removal man

Window cleaner

Gardener

Chauffeur

9 Before Matt paints the walls, Mick covers them with plaster. It is a tricky job. Mick works fast to use the plaster he has mixed before it dries.

8 The house is nearly ready, but it still needs electricity. Lotta Light, the electrician, puts in all the wiring, the plugs and light fittings.

5 The walls of the house are built of bricks and mortar. Bill Ditt, the bricklayer uses a spirit level and string to make sure the wall is level.

6 Tim Burr makes the door and window frames out of wood. When the brickwork is finished, he will build a wooden roof frame.

7 The carpenter's job is done. Now Hugh Bend, the plumber, fits the pipes for hot and cold water to the kitchen, bathrooms and water tanks.

The Hotel Keeper

It is a busy day at the Hotel Blitz, the smartest hotel in Banilla. Carmen Stay, the hotel keeper, is getting it ready for the famous rock group, Gracie and the Grumbles.

This evening, Carmen is giving a big banquet for the group. There is much to do before they arrive. Carmen goes round the hotel to tell her staff what she would like them to prepare.

Gracie will sleep in the best bedroom at the Blitz. The chambermaid makes the bed and cleans the room.

Gracie's fans have sent her lots of flowers. Carmen asks the housekeeper to put them all in pretty vases.

In the bathroom, Carmen checks that there is soap, perfume and clean towels.

The tables in the banquet room are being laid with the finest glass and cutlery. Each one is decorated with Banilla orchids.

Carmen asks the barman, Phil McLass, to mix a special cocktail for drinks before the party.

In the lobby, Carmen tells everyone what to do when the group arrives. Hugo Ferst, the doorman, waits outside.

Carmen is delighted with the food her head chef, Gordon Blurr, has cooked for the banquet. The lobster soup is delicious.

The Grumbles arrive

Everything is ready when the car drives up with Gracie and the Grumbles.

People have come from all over the island to cheer them. The group is very popular in Banilla.

In the kitchen

In the kitchen, Gordon Blurr and his cooks have almost finished preparing the feast for tonight.

One of the underchefs is in bad trouble. He has forgotten to make a special sauce.

The banquet

The banquet is a great success, the food and wine delicious. Gracie and the Grumbles thank Carmen Stay and Gordon Blurr.

Menu
Lobster Soup
Baked Fish in cream
Fresh Vegetables
Banilla icecream with chocolate sauce

The hotel staff

Hotel keeper

Housekeeper

Chambermaids   Valets

Receptionist

Door-man   Hall porter   Bell-boy

Barman   Restaurant manager

Head Chef

Underchefs

Waiters and Waitresses

The School Teacher

Les Chatter is one of the teachers at Noah Lott School in Banilla. About fifty children, aged from five to eight, go to the school. Les teaches them to read, write, spell and act.

He has been teaching on the island for almost ten years now, helping Miss Chief, the headmistress, to run the school. One day he hopes to be a headmaster himself.

Headmistress

Miss Chief is in charge of the school.

Les Chatter is the deputy headmaster. He teaches English.

Deputy Head

Maths Teacher

Gemma Tree teaches the children number work and sums.

Sue Prano teaches music, singing and the piano.

Music Teacher

Art Teacher

Walter Culler teaches drawing, painting and pottery.

Denise Bent takes the children for games and gym.

Gym Teacher

Les Chatter's day at school

9.30 a.m.

At the beginning of each day, Les Chatter marks the register to check that all his pupils are in the classroom.

11.00 a.m.

After an English lesson, Les lets the class rehearse for the school play. Billy Bunn will be the king.

12.30 p.m.

At dinner, Les sits at the top of the table. Today there is chicken, peas and potatoes. Every scrap must be eaten.

3.00 p.m.

It is games time. Les Chatter's team, in the red bands, is racing against Denise Bent's team, in the green bands.

4.30 p.m.

At the end of a tiring day, Les Chatter has a rest in the staffroom and a drink of special Banilla tea.

Midnight

There is still work to be done at home. After supper, Les marks homework and prepares more lessons.

Noah Lott School

Twice a week, after lessons, the school choir practises with Sue Prano in the music room.

The best painting this week will be entered for the Banilla art competition.

Today, a student teacher is telling the nature class about Banilla frogs.

There are some good gymnasts at this school. They will give a gym display at the end of term.

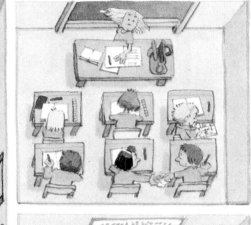

Librarian

Everyone has to be very quiet in the school library.

Cleaner

Groundsman

Every day, the groundsman brings in fresh flowers to decorate the hall.

School Secretary

Miss Chief asks the school secretary to invite Mayor Naze and her husband to the gym display.

13

The Baker

Master Baker

Bob Bunn is a master baker. He owns the Bunn Bakery in Banilla. Bob's father started the bakery 50 years ago. When he retired, Bob took over the business from him.

Baker

Bob's own daughter, Cherry Bunn, works with him now. For four years she was an apprentice at the bakery. Cherry still has much to learn before she becomes a master baker, too.

Pastry maker

Mike Doe is an expert pastry maker. He has won many awards with his famous Banilla cream puffs. Mike was trained by Pierre Pouff, a pastry maker in Paris.

Cake decorator

Maisie Pann came to live in Banilla when she was 16. She has worked for Bob ever since, decorating all the cakes, buns, tarts and pastries.

Bob, Cherry, Mike and Maisie start work at 3.30 every morning. By lunch, nearly all the baking is done.

Cake mixing machine

Proving oven

The pastry room

Mike makes all kinds of delicious pastries. He fills them with fruit and Banilla cream.

The doughnut room

The doughnuts are fried in bins of hot oil. Then they are filled with jam and cream.

Baking oven

Cooling racks

Bread mixing machine

Apprentice Baker

Making bread

1 Cherry Bunn makes the dough with flour, fat, yeast and water. She puts it all together in a big mixing machine.

2 She cuts the dough into small pieces and weighs each piece.

3 The lumps of dough are made into different-shaped loaves.

4 Then the loaves are put into a warm oven called a prover which makes them rise.

5 They are baked in another very hot oven until the tops are crusty and golden brown.

The decorating room

Today, Maisie Pann has a special job to do. She is icing a big wedding cake. Carmen Stay and Les Chatter are getting married on Saturday.

The bakery shop

Shopkeeper

Some of the bread, cakes, pastries and buns are sold in the bakery shop. The rest are delivered, before breakfast, to shops, hotels, restaurants and homes.

The Farmer

Daisy Fields is a dairy farmer. At Daisychain Farm, she keeps a herd of 50 milking cows. She also rears pigs to sell for pork, ham and bacon, and lots of egg-laying chickens.

It is hard work running a big farm, but Daisy has six strong people to help her. Each of them has a special job to do.

The farmworkers

Farm Manager

Dairy Woman

Herdsman

Pigman

Poultry keeper

Tractor driver

Daisychain Farm

The herdsman, Ron Dermupp, brings the cows in from the fields at milking time.

Ivan Aker, the farm manager, helps Daisy Fields run the farm. He is in charge of the farm workers.

Daisy is thinking about the five cows she hopes to buy at the cattle market this afternoon.

The poultry yard

Henrietta Negg, the poultry keeper, looks after the chickens. Every morning, she collects their eggs, sorts them into sizes and takes them off to sell at market. At night, she makes sure the hens are safe in the henhouse.

16

Carter Bowt is the tractor driver. He does all sorts of jobs on the farm.

Early each morning and evening, Phillipa Pale, the dairywoman, milks the cows in the milking parlour.

The milk from the bottles is pumped to a big storage tank.

Every day, a big milk tanker comes to collect the milk from the farm.

The special food Phillipa gives the cows helps them to make more milk.

It takes Phillipa over three hours to milk all the cows and clean the parlour.

Phillipa knows all the cows by name.

The piggery

The pigman, Frank Furter, looks after the pigs. Today, a sow is ill. Mike Atsil, the vet, has come to see what is wrong.

Frank likes his pigs. Everyday, he cleans out their pens and gives them plenty to eat so that they grow fat fast.

The Garage Owner

Gus O'Lean owns the biggest and busiest garage in Banilla. People come from all over the island to buy his cars. In the workshop, his mechanics mend punctures, change tyres and repair cars which have broken down or have been smashed in bad accidents.

They often go out with the breakdown lorry to tow damaged cars back to the garage. Gus's carwash is the best one in Banilla. It cleans and waxes cars until they sparkle. His garage shop is stocked full of oil, grease, polish, batteries and tyres for his customers to buy.

The workshop

In the noisy workshop, Jackie Tupp, the mechanic, has a special job to do today. Ray Strack, the famous racing driver, wants her to tune his car for the Banilla Grand Prix next week.

The storeroom

Fanny Belt, the storeroom manager, makes sure there are lots of spare parts in stock to fit all kinds of cars.

The paintshop

Dwight Spirit, the paintshop manager, and his assistant wear masks when they spray cars with paint.

Garage owner

Service manager

Secretary

Sales manager

Saleswoman

Mechanics

Gus O'Lean buys new cars from a factory on the mainland. He only buys old cars from other dealers that are in good working order.

The service manager, Nellie Dunn, books cars into the workshop. She tells her customers how much the repairs will cost.

Dick Tate is Gus's secretary. He types letters and helps with important office work.

The showroom

Otto Mattick is the sales manager at the garage. He and Emma Chizzit, the saleswoman, sell new and second-hand cars in the showroom.

Emma has just sold a two-seater sports car to Daisy Fields, the farmer. In front of the showroom are the petrol pumps and garage shop.

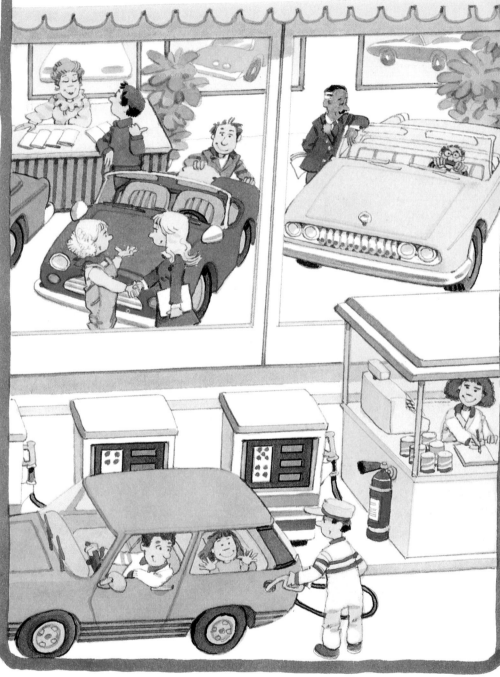

Stores manager

Paintshop manager

Paintshop assistant

Receptionist

Car cleaners

Petrol pump attendant

Shop keeper

19

The Newspaper Reporter

Weaver Scoop is a reporter for the Banilla Daily Blaze newspaper. He writes stories about the people on the island and all the exciting things that happen there.

Like all good reporters, Weaver works hard to find interesting things to write about. He is good at asking people questions and finding out about their lives.

Three other reporters, Wanda Farr, Dennis Court and Justine Vogue work at the paper, too. They have special subjects to write about. Len Scap is the photographer.

General Reporter

As well as reporting in Banilla, Weaver goes abroad to give talks about the island and all the people who live there.

Foreign Reporter

Wanda Farr travels around the world to report on things that happen in other countries.

Fashion Reporter

Justine Vogue writes all the fashion stories. She goes to lots of fashion shows.

Sports Reporter

Dennis Court loves sport. He writes about golf, athletics, tennis and motor racing.

Photographer

Len Scap takes good pictures. He goes to everything that happens on the island.

The editor-in-chief's office

Editor-in-chief →

Secretary

News Editor ↓

Messenger ↙

The editor-in-chief, Ivor Hunch, is the boss at the Daily Blaze. Every day, he reads all the stories the reporters write and decides which ones to print in the newspaper.

Eva Penn, the news editor, is in charge of the reporters. Early each morning, she talks to them about the stories they will write for the next day's edition of the Daily Blaze.

A fashion show

Fashion model →

At a fashion show, Justine Vogue writes about the latest fashions of the top dress designer, Ellie Gant.

Abroad

Wanda Farr, on a nearby island, has a sad story to report. A whale has been beached. Will it survive?

The big race

Racing driver ↙

Dennis Court interviews the famous racing driver, Ray Strack. He has just won the Banilla Grand Prix.

20

The wedding

Weaver Scoop is reporting on one of the biggest events of the year — the marriage between Carmen Stay, the hotel keeper, and Les Chatter, the school teacher.

When the speeches have all been made, Weaver hurries back to his office to write about the wedding. Len's best photographs will be printed with his story.

The sub-editor

The sub-editor looks at and corrects Weaver's story. She makes sure that he has not made any grammar or spelling mistakes.

The keyboard operator

Then the keyboard operator types the story into a computer. This produces columns of type on long strips of paper.

The compositor

The compositor's job is to paste up the strips of type to make up the pages of the newspaper. Printing plates are made for each page.

The machine room

Machine minder

Every evening, thousands of newspapers are printed on a big printing press. It is a hot, hard and noisy job for the machine minders. As soon as the papers are printed, they are delivered around the island.

The Daily Blaze

Weaver Scoop is delighted. His wedding story has made the headlines. It has been printed on the front page of tomorrow's Daily Blaze.

21

The Pilot

Captain Charlie Tango is an airline pilot. He works for Banilla Airways and flies big jet aeroplanes with lots of passengers all over the world. On every flight there is a co-pilot. Today, Joyce Tick will help Captain Tango fly the plane to Orly Airport in France.

Roger Tower is also aboard Banilla Airways flight 333. He is the flight engineer. His job is to make sure the jet works perfectly. It is a long trip to France. On the way, the plane will stop once to re-fuel. The crew will spend a night in Paris before flying home.

The flight crew

Pilot Co-pilot Flight Engineer

Captain Tango and his crew check in at the airport two hours before the plane takes off. There is work to be done.

The weather desk

Weather forecaster

First, at the weather desk, the Captain gets a report of the weather conditions on the route he is flying today.

The operations room

He then makes out a flight plan to show the route he is taking, how high and at what speed he will fly the jet.

Before take-off

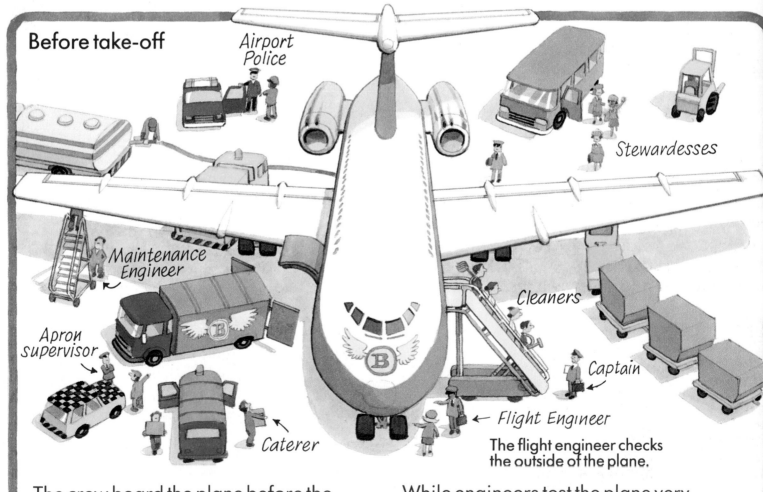

Airport Police

Stewardesses

Maintenance Engineer

Apron supervisor

Cleaners

Captain

Caterer

Flight Engineer

The flight engineer checks the outside of the plane.

The crew board the plane before the passengers. As soon as it is cleaned, all the food and drink is brought on board and the luggage and cargo is loaded.

While engineers test the plane very carefully to make sure it is safe to fly, thousands of litres of fuel are pumped into the big tanks in the wings of the plane.

The flight deck

The Captain, co-pilot and flight engineer sit inside the flight deck at the front of the plane. Before taking off, they check all the flying controls and instruments to make sure they are working well.

Boarding the plane

Chief Stewardess

Rock group

The chief stewardess welcomes Gracie and the Grumbles aboard flight 333. During the flight, the stewardesses make sure all the passengers are comfortable and serve them with food and drink.

The control tower

Ground control officer

Everything is ready. The passengers are safely strapped into their seats. The doors are closed. Captain Tango radios the control tower and asks permission to start the jet engines and taxi down the runway.

At the end of the runway, Captain Tango moves the wing flaps of the big jet into position, opens up the throttles and speeds down the runway. The plane rises smoothly into the air. Banilla Airways flight 333 is off.

When the plane is safely in the air, Captain Tango tells his passengers all about the journey ahead.

During the flight, he goes into the passenger cabin to wish Mr and Mrs Chatter a happy honeymoon in Paris.

Now it is time to land. Right on time, Captain Tango touches down on the runway at Orly Airport.

The Fire Brigade

The Station Commander, Ivor Hose, is in charge of the Banilla fire brigade. His men call him 'the Chief'. Ivor is the most important person at the fire station.

Fire Chief

Sub-officer

Mandy Pumps is second-in-command. She helps Ivor run the fire brigade. Mandy often goes out with the firemen to help put out big fires.

The two leading firemen, Don Pannick and José Bilding are in charge of all the firemen and women. Every morning, they tell them their duties and in which fire engines they will be riding.

Leading Firemen

The rest of the brigade is made up of ordinary firemen and women. There are twenty of them in the Banilla brigade.

Firemen and Firewomen

24

Keeping fit

All firemen and women have to be fit and strong and learn how to work well as a team. Every day they do all kinds of hard exercises to strengthen their muscles.

The Banilla fire station

A big fire is burning at the Daily Blaze Newspaper office. Firemen with two fire engines have already left the station to fight the fire. But more firemen are needed urgently to help.

The firemen stop whatever they are doing when they hear the fire alarm go.

Station Cook

They hurry down to the fire engine room as fast as they possibly can.

Duty officer

In the control room, the duty officer talks by radio to Ivor Hose at the fire.

FIRE ENGINE ROOM

As they drive to the burning building, the firemen change into their fire kit inside the fire engine. Not a moment must be wasted. It will take six minutes to reach the Daily Blaze.

An emergency

The Banilla fire brigade is always ready for an emergency. At fire drill practice, they spend hours learning how to put out fires and rescue people.

They learn how to put up and climb long ladders, how to use breathing equipment in thick smoke and how to carry heavy people over their shoulders.

The fire at the Daily Blaze is burning fiercely. But the firemen from the Banilla brigade do not panic. They will soon put out the fire.

Two people have been overcome by smoke. An ambulance is ready to take them off to hospital.

Firemen know all about first aid. They often have to help people who are hurt in fires.

Ambulance woman

Firemen attach a fire hose to a hydrant to draw water from a big underground pipe.

Ivor Hose has been hurt.

Reporter

THE DAILY BLAZE

Fireman Pannick has to hold on to the fire hose tightly to stop it from jumping out of his hands.

As well as fighting fires, the Banilla brigade sometimes have to rescue people from crashed cars and flooded places.

The Doctor

Doctor Penny Sillin has her own surgery in the town square. She also works at the hospital in Banilla.

Every morning, except on Sundays, ill people come to see her. In the afternoons, she goes to Saint Havedoc Hospital to visit her patients there. Sometimes, if people are very ill or badly hurt, Doctor Sillin has to operate on them.

The surgery

At the end of a busy day in her surgery, Doctor Sillin gets an urgent call from the hospital. Ivor Hose, the fire chief, has had an accident. He has broken his leg. Can she come quickly?

Scrubbing up

The doctor and her assistant wear clean gowns and masks. They scrub themselves with soap to get rid of any germs.

An anaesthetic

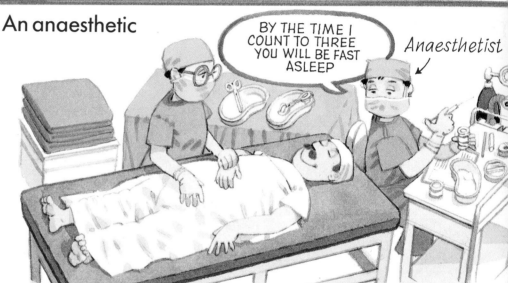

BY THE TIME I COUNT TO THREE YOU WILL BE FAST ASLEEP

Anaesthetist

Just before the operation, the anaesthetist, Arthur Sleep, gives Ivor Hose a big injection in his arm. Now he will sleep soundly while Doctor Sillin mends his broken leg.

The maternity ward

There is a lot of excitement in the maternity ward today. Mrs Bunn, the baker's wife, has just had triplets — two boys and a girl.

Len Scap has come to take pictures of the Bunn babies for his newspaper, the Daily Blaze.

The midwife, Linda Hand, helped to deliver the babies.

Midwife

On her daily rounds, Doctor Penny Sillin visits all the mothers and their new babies.

An x-ray

Radiographer

IT'S A VERY BAD BREAK, IVOR

While he waits for the doctor to arrive, Ivor has his leg x-rayed by the radiographer.

Ivor's leg is badly broken in two places. Doctor Sillin must operate on it at once.

Getting ready

Nurse

Nurse Patience gets Ivor ready for the operation. An injection will make him sleepy.

The operating theatre

Operating team

Everyone is quiet in the operating theatre as the doctor cuts open Ivor's leg. She joins the broken bones together and stitches up the wound. Next she will cover it in a plaster cast.

In the ward

Ivor wakes up in the ward. He is feeling much better and can have visitors now.

Father

Mother

Ward Sister

Sister Mattick is in charge of the maternity ward.

Porter

Another baby is about to be born.

Nurse

27

The Television Producer

Sonja Screen is a television producer. She is in charge of making a television programme called Ripples. Every week a new episode is shown on Banilla television.

Television Producer

Television Director

Roland Shoot, the director, is in charge of the actors and the people who work the camera, lighting and sound equipment. He tells them what to do.

Floor manager
Production assistant

Fay Dowt and Stan Still work with the director and help him with the actors.

Set Designer

Art Tiztik draws pictures of what he wants each scene to look like and makes models of them. Carpenters build full-size sets exactly like the models.

Actors

The producer and director choose the actors for the series. Oscar Winna and Carrie Zmatik will play the leading roles.

Making 'Ripples' — a television series

It is Sonja Screen's job to raise enough money to make the programmes. Then she hires all the people to work on Ripples.

Some of the scenes are filmed outside or 'on location'. But most of Ripples is filmed inside a big television studio.

1

Script writer

The story of Ripples has been written by a script writer. The script tells the actors what to say and what movements to make.

2

The actors practise each scene again and again. They read from the script to learn by heart their words and movements.

3

Art shows Sonja a model of the set for this week's episode. It has been made to look like the living room of a big house.

4

Propman

He tells the propman which things he needs for each scene. This week he wants furniture and lamps, carpets and pictures.

5

Wardrobe mistress
Leading Actress

The wardrobe mistress has made Carrie's dress especially for her. Carrie tries it on to make sure it fits her well.

6

In the dressing room, the make-up artist fits on a wig and false moustache to make the actor look much older.

In the studio

Ripples is a story about a rich family called the Zorbays who own lots of orchid plantations. The seed pods from the orchids are used to flavour Banilla ice cream.

This week, the Zorbays meet at the family mansion. Someone has tried to shoot Max Zorbay. Was it his wife or sister, Zelda? Everyone is quiet as filming begins.

Strong floodlights hang above the set to light it.

The microphone is on the end of a long rod called a boom.

IT WAS YOU. YOU WANTED ME TO DIE !

Boom operator

Camera man

The floor manager and cameramen listen to the director's instructions through their headphones.

Stan Still checks that everything is in the right place.

Sound Control room

Production Control room

Vision Control room

The director sits in the production control room with Fay Dowt. They speak through microphones to the people in the studio and in the vision and sound control rooms.

In the control rooms, engineers work the studio lights and the microphones. They make sure that the picture being filmed is clear and sharp and that the sound is good.

The Banilla Police

Police chief Colin Alcars is in charge of the police force in Banilla. Thirty officers help him look after the people on the island. They are trained to do all kinds of jobs — direct the traffic, look for missing people and animals, and help at fires and accidents.

The Banilla police work hard for many hours each day. They take it in turns to work at night. Sometimes they have to track down and catch a crook. Today, Chief Alcars has been called to Itchicoo Park. A thief has stolen the bronze statue of Mayor Naze.

Itchicoo Park

The police chief talks to a witness who says he saw the thief.

Sergeant Luke Hare reports progress back to police headquarters.

Patrol officer

Police chief

Witness

Police Sergeant

Detective Prue Vit hunts for a clue that might help her to find the crook.

Detective

Photographer

Fingerprint expert

Officer Hans Upp takes notes of everything the witness says.

A fingerprint expert finds two blurred fingerprints. Do they belong to the thief?

A police photographer takes pictures of anything that may be used as evidence.

Detective work

Detective Prue Vit studies fingerprints that were taken from near the statue.

She talks to one of the witnesses. He says the thief was fat and had red hair.

Prue helps the witness to remember more about the crook. What was he wearing? How tall was he? She uses a photofit kit to make up different faces. Was it Robin Banks?

River police

Two police frogmen rescue a man who has fallen into the Banilla river.

Dog handlers

Dog handler

Thief

Some police officers have dogs to help them track down and catch crooks.

The police station

At the police station, officer-in-charge, Eamonn Dooty, checks the cells.

Lots of people have come to see what has happened. Police officers on horses are helping to control the rowdy crowd.

Mounted Policeman

These children are lost. The policeman will take them home.

Mayor Naze is very upset. She is thinking about the stolen statue. Last year, the people of Banilla had it made in honour of all the good work she has done for them.

Inspector

Inspector Ann Cuff questions three more people who think they saw the thief.

This policeman is helping someone who has fainted. Police officers must know all about first aid.

She checks the criminal files. The fingerprints found match Robin's prints.

Prue tracks Robin down. He planned to melt the statue and sell the bronze.

She arrests the crook and handcuffs him. Then she takes him to the station.

Robin is put into a cell. Tomorrow he will be tried in court by the judge.

The Vet

Mike Atsil is a vet. For four years, he trained on the mainland. He learned how to mend broken bones, stitch wounds and give inoculations. He often performs operations and has saved the lives of many pets.

People in Banilla bring their sick pets to him to treat. Every morning and evening, two trained nurses help him at his busy surgery. In the afternoons, he goes to see all kinds of ill animals on farms nearby.

Veterinary Nurse
Vet

Receptionist

The vet is always on duty. People ring him at home if they are worried about their pets — even in the middle of the night.

Mike Atsil starts work at eight o'clock each day. Before his patients arrive, he checks that everything he needs is ready at the surgery.

The nurse writes down the name of each animal and what is wrong with it. Mayor Naze has brought her rabbit, Snuffles, to the surgery.

The waiting room

Carmen Stay's cat, Leo, has got bad earache.

Glitter, the goldfish has a badly torn fin.

Miss Chief's tortoise, Plod, has been bitten by a dog.

Slither, the snake, has got indigestion.

Hero, the police puppy, has come for an inoculation.

By nine o'clock, there are many people with their pets waiting to see the vet.

Mike Atsil knows how to treat all kinds of different animals, fish and birds.

32

In the surgery

The vet sees Snuffles first. He looks at her teeth, eyes, ears and mouth. And then he listens to her breathing and heartbeat through a stethoscope.

The rabbit has a bad cold. Mike gives her an injection to help her to get better. He tells Mayor Naze to keep Snuffles warm and that she should be much better in a week.

Visiting Daisychain Farm

Farmer

In the afternoon, Mike drives to Daisy Field's Farm. Her horse, Trot, is lame. The vet finds that Trot has corns and needs new shoes.

He then looks at the sow he gave medicine to last week. She is much better now and will probably have her piglets soon.

Mike visits two more farms before he goes back to the surgery. He has plenty of medicines in his car.

At evening surgery, Peter, the parrot, is Mike's first patient. The parrot has come to have its long claws clipped.

Surgery is over, but the vet still has work to do. He writes down all the treatments and visits he has done today.

The Ballet Dancer

Ballerina

Barre practice

Ballet dancers

Ballet mistress

Pianist

Honor Toze and Leo Tarde are Banilla's leading ballet dancers. They have both been dancing since they were five years old. Before they joined the Banilla Ballet Company, they went to a ballet school.

Every morning, they go to ballet classes to practise their steps and to exercise their muscles. In the afternoon, they rehearse for the evening performance of the ballet they are to dance.

First the dancers practise at the barre. They stretch and bend to warm up their muscles. Dancers work hard to keep fit and strong.

The ballet mistress, Diane Swann, was a famous ballerina. She teaches the dancers their exercises and corrects their mistakes.

A rehearsal

Conductor

Choreographer

Orchestra

Pierre O'Wet is a choreographer. His job is to create new ballets for the Banilla Company to dance. First he chooses the music for the ballet. Then he works out all the steps and movements he wants the dancers to do.

At rehearsals, the dancers try out Pierre's latest ballet. He shows them all exactly what to do. After many weeks of practice they know their steps perfectly. The Banilla orchestra plays at the last few rehearsals.

Centre work

After barre practice, the dancers do the exercises in the middle of the floor. They learn jumps and turning steps, and how to hold their arms, hands and heads. Ballet dancers must look graceful all the time.

Double work

Honor and Leo dance together for many hours each day. They have been partners now for nearly six years. Leo practises holding and supporting Honor. He does all kinds of difficult lifts and catches.

Getting ready

Wardrobe mistress

BEGINNERS ON STAGE PLEASE

Wig master   *Stage manager*

It is almost time for the ballet to begin. In the dressing room, the dancers put on their make-up and get into their costumes. Kurt Nupp, the stage manager, tells them that they must be ready to go on stage in five minutes' time.

The performance

At the end of the performance, all the dancers take a bow. The audience loved Pierre's ballet. They clapped for ten minutes and threw flowers on to the stage. Honor Toze, who danced beautifully, is presented with a big bouquet.

35

The Banilla Festival

Every year there is a big festival in Banilla to celebrate the Mayor's birthday. People from all over the island, come to Itchicoo Park to join in the fun and excitement.

There are singing and dancing competitions, raffles and races, lots of prizes to win and delicious food to eat.

Look for the people you have already met in this book. Can you remember their names?

Ivor Hose is judging the cake competition. He likes Cherry Bunn's chocolate and cream cake the best.

This year Honor Toze and Leo Tarde will choose the best rock and rollers in the dancing competition.

All the food has been made by Carmen Stay and her hotel chefs.

The guest-of-honour, Mayor Naze, has arrived. Walter Wall, the carpet layer, rolls out the red carpet for her.

BLITZ

HAPPY BIRTHDAY

BANILLA ICE CREAM

BEST CAKE COMPETITION

FLOUNDER'S FISH

Gracie and the Grumbles give a concert of their latest hit songs at every festival. Sonja Screen is filming it to show on Banilla television.

MAYOR NAZE

GRACIE AND THE GRUMBLES

RAFFLE Tickets

DAISYCHAIN FARM FRUIT

BUNN IS BEST

Judge Fairley is very happy. He has just won the first prize in the festival raffle.

Who will win the tug-of-war today? Will it be Manuel Laber and his builders or the fire brigade team?

RACES

PET OF THE YEAR

Who will be pet of the year?

Captain Charlie Tango presents the winners of the three-legged race with their medals.

Index